MAKE ART
KAWAII

Written by
ELLEN PHILPOTT

Illustrated by
ILARIA RANAURO

CONTENTS

What is kawaii art?	4
Kawaii all around us	6
What is a chibi?	8
Play with proportions	10
Express yourself!	12
Get ahead	14
Step-by-step people	16
Keeping it real	18
Walk on the wild side	20
Cute and cuddly pets	22

From creepy to cute	24
Fabulous & funny food	26
Out and about: the natural world	28
The everyday comes alive	30
Spooky & sweet	32
Making characters	34
Backgrounds & backdrops	36
Details & decorations	38
Color palettes	40
Kawaii creations: make it move!	42
Kawaii creations: peekaboo!	44
Kawaii creations: make it pop!Es	46

WHAT IS KAWAII ART?

Kawaii means "cute" or "adorable", and it is a style that originally came from Japan. It features adorable characters with sweet faces that make you feel tenderness and warmth when you look at them. They might be people, animals, or even objects, drawn with a simplified and rounded shape. They make you want to pick them up for a hug!

The cute style began when teenage girls started writing in a rounded way with added hearts, stars, and faces. This made the teachers mad, and it was even banned in many schools! But once the trend had begun, it was unstoppable.

Hello Kitty, one of the most famous kawaii characters, was launched in 1974 and was a huge worldwide hit. Soon, other characters came along and captured people's hearts.

These days, kawaii characters are so popular they can be found all over the world on stationery, plush toys, food products, and clothes. Even emojis were influenced by the kawaii style!

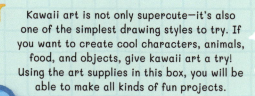

Kawaii art is not only supercute—it's also one of the simplest drawing styles to try. If you want to create cool characters, animals, food, and objects, give kawaii art a try! Using the art supplies in this box, you will be able to make all kinds of fun projects.

HOW IS IT DRAWN?

Kawaii art uses simple shapes and lines to create cute characters with lovable faces, small characters with big heads, and adorable faces.

Often, the eyes, nose, and mouth are close together in the center of the face, giving a childlike, innocent appearance.

There are no sharp edges—everything is soft and rounded. Soothing and uplifting colors are used—think pastels and rainbows!

ACTIVITY: MY CUTE ROOM!

Make your room kawaii-stylish by adding a cute door hanger from your kit. Color it in, add some stickers, and fill in your name.
Now pop it on your door!

KAWAII ALL AROUND US

Kawaii might have started out as a trend for teenagers, but soon it became popular with people of all ages. Big companies started to use kawaii characters as a part of their branding, and this helped to spread its popularity around the world. Now, kawaii style can be seen on everything from toys to kitchenware. There is even a Hello Kitty train and a fleet of Pokemon airplanes! 素晴らしい Subarashii! (Awesome!)

FASHION FAVORITES

Kawaii fashion means dressing in a cute way, with colorful, frilly clothes, lace, and bows. A Tokyo district called Harajuku is known as the epicenter of kawaii style.

Harajuku

"Lolita" fashion is one type of kawaii style which involves cute dresses, frills, and ruffles.

Another style is "Decora", which involves wearing a ton of accessories such as jewelery and hair clips.

EVENTS

Fans can get together at conventions to celebrate their love of kawaii culture. Comic-Con is one of the events where you can meet your favorite characters and buy merch! It's also an opportunity to go all out and dress up with fellow fans.

PRODUCT POWER

There are so many amazing kawaii products you can buy! Toys (especially squishy plush toys), lamps, backpacks, jewelery, cable holders, fidget toys, and flowerpots are just a few.

ACTIVITY: BE A FASHION DESIGNER

Press out the dress-up-dolly figure from your kit. Now find the kawaii dress-up stickers. Channel your inner stylist and put together a cool kawaii outfit. Don't forget to add accessories! いいね Suteki! That means cool.

WHAT IS A CHIBI?

A "chibi" is a character drawn in the chibi art style. This is a fun style of drawing that is usually found in anime, manga, and video games.

Chibis are similar to caricatures, but always tiny and cute. They have simplified bodies and exaggerated features. If you've seen Astro Boy, Chibiusa, or Teen Titans then you have seen chibi art!

BIG FEELINGS, SMALL CHIBI!

Sometimes, a chibi version of a character will **POP** up for a scene in an anime movie. This is used for emphasis and for comedy effect—because the character is feeling strong emotions.

すごい Sugoi! (Wow!)

SPOT THE DIFFERENCE

See how this anime-style character switches into a cute chibi with just a few changes.

- Simple arms with no hands or fingers
- Detailed body and clothes
- Accessories are BIG
- Soft, pastel colors

- Bigger head
- HUGE eyes
- Smaller body
- Simple legs and feet
- Clothes are more rounded

8

ACTIVITY: CHIBI FUN!

Turn this superhero into a fun chibi in the space below.

Otsu! Good work today!

Now find the chibi sheet in your set.
Practice turning each character into a chibi!

PLAY WITH PROPORTIONS

When you are learning to draw figures, you need to know about proportions. Traditionally, artists make the head about one-eighth of the height of the body.

In kawaii art, we change it up! Kawaii characters always have **BIG** heads compared with their bodies. But within this style, there are different approaches. It's fun to try them all and see which one you like best.

SAME SIZE HEAD AND BODY

Emiko the bear is drawn in **50/50** proportion. Her head is the same size as her body. Start with two circles and then add ears, paws, or any special characteristics. Try drawing a friend for Emiko in **50/50** proportion.

BIGGER HEAD THAN BODY

Kawaii is such a fun, exaggerated style that it doesn't have to play by the rules. Your character's head can be even bigger than their body. This can look really cute.

Mai the dancer is drawn in **70/30** proportion. This means that only 30% of her height is her body and the rest is her head. Try drawing a friend for her to dance with.

ALL BODY!

This is a really popular choice for kawaii art—there is no separate head at all! The face is drawn as part of the body. The only definition is little details like feet or ears.

It sounds crazy but it works! This is also why so many objects can be kawaii—they become a character without having to be shaped like a person.

Saikou! 最高

ACTIVITY!

Take the "Play with Proportions" stencil from your set and add some 100% proportion characters to the scene below. Don't forget to give each character a cute face!

EXPRESS YOURSELF!

Kawaii characters often have a round and cuddly shape. Their faces are often big compared to bodies, similar to the proportions of a baby's face, and it makes them look cute! Their eyes, noses, when one is included, and mouths are quite close together. Make your character look distinctive by adding expressions!

It's easy to change an expression by tweaking the eyebrows and mouth. Try copying these expressions onto Mio the Bunny below.

TURN THAT FROWN UPSIDE DOWN!

HAPPY — Carrot cake! Yummy.

SAD — Oh no! I dropped my cookie on the floor.

ANGRY — Hey! Who stepped on my fluffy tail?

EXCITED — It's the bunny disco tonight! I'm going to bunny hop 'til I drop!

HI, I'M MIO!

FIND YOUR STYLE

It's fun to experiment with different styles for features. Eyes can be drawn as simple dots or they can be curved or angular to indicate different emotions. Copy these super cute features onto Una the Unicorn below.

CUTE — I love you more than ice cream!
SHY — Um, can I play with you?
THRILLED — Wheee! I love zip lining!
SASSY — You can't catch me...ever!

HI, I'M UNA!

PET BOXES

1. FOLD 2. STICK 3. DRAW

- Take the paper box template and fold along the lines.
- Stick the colored tabs to the sides to make a box shape.
- Turn your box into a friendly animal by adding features. Add little pieces of curved cardstock stuck to the box lid to make ears that stick up!

Variation: For extra fun, decorate each side of the box with a different expression!

Now your animal pals can keep your erasers, paper clips, and hair clips safe for you.

GET AHEAD!

Let's focus on heads for a moment. You've seen how kawaii heads can be really big in proportion to the body. It's also useful to practice drawing heads from different angles, so you can show your characters doing different things.

星Hoshi!'—that means star!

HEADS UP!

Take a simple drawing of a face. If we add a pencil line down the center and another across the eyeline, (cross-contour lines) we can then play around with how the face looks at different angles. Let's add some ears as well, so we can see how they would move with the head.

Look down—You just stepped in a puddle!

Look up! That cloud is shaped like a unicorn!

Now go this way . . . and that way . . .

You can draw your character in any direction!

I see some bamboo—yummy!

You can do exactly the same thing with a cute animal face. This panda has round ears.

GOOD HAIR DAY

Try out a couple of basic hair styles too, and think about how they would move with your character.

ACTIVITY: FINGER PUPPETS

Now you try! Find the finger puppet sheet. Add a cute face to the koala and the lion. Fold the tabs and glue them to the back of the puppet. Now you're ready to play puppets!

楽しい
Tanoshii!
That means fun!

STEP-BY-STEP PEOPLE

Let's take a closer look at how to draw kawaii-style people. You can make your pictures more interesting by drawing people in varied poses, such as waving or running.

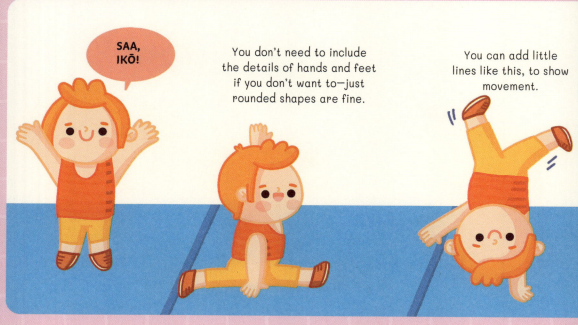

Now let's try making people look different by giving them clothes and props. You can tell what all these characters do by the things they are wearing and using.

SASSY CHEF

This little chef has made some yummy pizza. Oishii! 美味しい That means delicious!

Draw the head and body shapes.

Add in the chef's hat and hair!

Add clothes, face, and pizza.

HER ROYAL KAWAII-NESS This princess has a fancy tiara!

Draw the head and dress shape.

Add the hair, tiara, and face.

Add the details of the dress.

DR. ADORABLE Draw this little doctor giving a friendly wave.

Draw the head and body shapes.

Ponytail and white coat detail.

Add face, stethoscope, and medical bag.

ACTIVITY: DOODLE ALL DAY!

Find the printed sheet of picture frames in your kit. Now practice drawing a different kawaii character in each frame. Don't worry about making them too neat, just relax and allow yourself to make mistakes!

17

KEEPING IT REAL

You've tried drawing lots of made-up characters. How about creating some pictures of real people? Think about who you'd like to draw. Maybe it's your friend, a family member, or your favorite singer. What are the things that make them special? Choose something about them that stands out and include it in your drawing.

YOUR GORGEOUS GALLERY

Try turning the outlines below into people you know. Do they have a cool ponytail, a sunny smile, or cute glasses? Drawing a friend who loves jewelery? Make their earrings and necklace stand out! Does your brother always make you laugh? Draw him with a big smile. It's best to pick just one or two things to emphasize and keep the rest of your design simple.

Draw on some clothes in your chosen person's style. Maybe they are obsessed with bright colors, or maybe they always wear black. Try to show real details that you've noticed about them.

MIRROR MIRROR ON THE WALL

Now take a look in the mirror! You're going to draw a kawaii selfie. In Japanese, that's jidori! 自撮り

How would you like your cute avatar to look? First, draw a rough draft. Look at your reflection in the mirror and try to sketch what you see. Then draw it in kawaii style, making sure to include your favorite accessories!

ACTIVITY: THE GIFT OF CUTENESS

Take the picture frame from your kit and make a gift for someone you love. Color in your frame, then draw a kawaii picture of the two of you together and place it in the frame. You'll make somebody's day!

BEST FRIENDS FOREVER

WALK ON THE WILD SIDE

Emi the red panda wants to see you draw! Wild animals are a great choice for kawaii art inspiration. Practice drawing these, then why not try drawing the most unusual animal you can think of. Maybe a quokka, or a capybara! Decorate your notebooks and make posters for your room featuring animals of all shapes and sizes.

JOYFUL GIRAFFE

For the giraffe, start with the head and draw a little arch across it. Include two small ears and two little horns.

Then of course, we need a nice long neck leading to the small body and legs. Add a little tail and a face.

Finally, give her some nice big spots.

MONKEY MAGIC

For the monkey, draw three circles first. Then draw a heartlike shape for the face outline.

Next, add a body and a long tail looping upward.

Give him some arms, legs, and a banana. Then add a sassy face.

LOVELY LION

Draw a round face shape and two cute ears. Then draw a frilly outline for the mane.

Add a body and rounded legs.

Finally, give your lion a friendly face and a sticking-up tail.

ELEGANT ELEPHANT

Let's start by drawing a large oval with some small legs.

Add two big, wavy ears.

Then finish by adding the curved trunk, the eyes, and the other two legs.

ACTIVITY: ORIGAMI LION

Find the press-out sheet in your kit.

Turn it over and fold each corner back along the dotted lines to make a face shape.

To make the ears, fold the top two corners back to the front along the orange line.

Turn the paper over, then draw a circle shape for the face.

5 Add mane and a cute lion face!

21

CUTE & CUDDLY PETS!

Kawaii art aims to make people feel emotions such as warmth and tenderness, so it's no surprise that soft, round-bodied pets are such a popular subject! Their little bodies and big heads with cute eyes make them extra adorable.

SUPERCUTE SOUNDS

Kawaii pet drawings sometimes include sweet animal noises. These can be shown as a word linked to the animal's mouth by a zigzag or wavy line, or in a speech bubble.

Nyan nyan! (ニャンニャン) is the sound of a cat's meow.

Wan wan! (ワンワン) is the sound of a dog's bark.

Pyon Pyon! (ピョンピョン) is the sound of a jumping bunny.

PRETTY KITTY!

Nyan nyan! With their soft fur and expressive eyes, cats are seen everywhere in Kawaii art.

Start by lightly drawing two circles for the head and body. These will be your guides.

Add some rounded ears, a cute face, and whiskers.

Finally, add tucked-in paws and some back leg definition, a curved tail, and a collar.

DOG POWER!

Wan wan! Kawaii dogs are often playful and cuddly, just like this one!

Start by lightly drawing an oval for the face and another one for the body.

Add two furry ears and a sweet face, with a cute tuft of fur on top.

Finally, add front paws, back legs, a tail, and a collar.

BOUNCING BUNNY!

Moe (萌え), a Japanese slang word for the feeling of adorable cuteness, is a perfect reaction to this sweet bunny!

Start by lightly drawing an oval head and a curved body. These will be your guides.

Draw ears, arms, and legs. This bunny is going to stand on two legs!

Finally, add facial features—whiskers, paw details, and a cute fluffy tail.

PENCIL TOPPERS

1. Find the pencil topper flags, then carefully cut them out.

2. Use your new skills to draw a pet on each flag and color in.

3. Fold each flag over and secure it with a piece of tape over the top of your favorite pencils. You'll have a friendly pal with you whenever you draw!

23

FROM CREEPY TO CUTE

Kawaii style has the power to change things from scary to cute! This is even true of creepy-crawlies—you can take a big spider and give it a smiley kawaii face and it will be transformed. Yes, even you, Fumiko Spider!

This beanstalk is growing from a magic bean. It reaches all the way up into the clouds. Look at the bugs and copy a different one onto each leaf.

BUTTERFLY

LADYBUG

SPIDER

GRASSHOPPER

WORM

MOVING

This snail has a really cute home on his back! Copy the picture into the box below.

APPLE ANTICS

Draw a friendly caterpillar crawling on top of the apple, and then give the apple a surprised face.

ACTIVITY: MAGICAL GARDEN

1 Press out the snail, butterfly, and flower pieces.

2 Use the stickers to add cute kawaii details to each model and decorate your scene.

3 Now draw some cute kawaii facial expressions on each model. Try happy, sad and silly.

4 Slot each model into to base and enjoy your mini garden!

FABULOUS & FUNNY FOOD

Kawaii food art is just so adorable. A cute combination of tasty treats and sweet faces—what's not to like? It's fun to take something we see every day and make it look more interesting. Food kawaii just makes everybody smile!

26

GRUMPY PASTA!

Copy this picture of an angry bowl of pasta. First, draw the bowl. Then add some twists of pasta to the top. Sprinkle on some little squares of chopped vegetables. Now give the bowl a grumpy face!

ACTIVITY: GROCERY SHOP MINIS

1 Find the food templates in your kit. There is a strawberry cake mix, an egg carton, and an orange juice carton to make.

2 Color in each template. Then add a cute little face.

3 Gently press out each template, and fold along the creases. Glue the tabs to the sides to form each box.

NOW SET UP YOUR OWN KAWAII STORE!

STRAWBERRY CAKE MIX **EGGS** **ORANGE JUICE**

OUT AND ABOUT: THE NATURAL WORLD

Nature has always been an inspiration for art. If you've ever visited a art museum, you have probably seen big landscape paintings of the ocean or of the country. Kawaii art also uses elements of the natural world.

There are some beautiful, simple outlines from nature that you can use to get started.

A leaf shape works well, or an acorn or cactus.

You can try a tree, a toadstool, or a moon shape.

Then of course there are the animals you will see when out in the country.

PRICKLY PAL

Draw this friendly cactus on the postcard

1. First, draw the pot and the rounded body. Add an arm on each side.
2. Make it prickly by adding lots of little spikes! Add a pretty flower.
3. Give her a friendly face.

WONDERFUL WOODS

Hi! I'm Hana Hedgehog! Look at this woods in this scene. Could you please add some more friends for me?

ACTIVITY: MAKE A ANIMAL CARD

1. Find the card template in your kit and fold it in half along the line. Write your greeting in large letters.

   This could be 'Happy Birthday!', 'Best Friend!', 'Well Done!' or anything else you like.

2. Now think of the person you are making the card for. Draw their favorite animal on the front of the card. Make it kawaii!

3. Color your card in and decorate it with stickers and stencils.

THE EVERYDAY COMES ALIVE

Kawaii art can take boring, everyday objects and make them look fun. Try it! Look around your home and find the most mundane item you can, then draw it in kawaii style. It'll be transformed! There's almost nothing that can't be made adorable with kawaii styling.

This is why you'll often see things like bowls, kettles, toasters, and notebooks made kawaii—we enjoy the contrast between their practical use and the playful and cute way they look.

KAWAII CLEANUP

Even chores are fun when you have kit like this! Draw on faces and then add a broom, a mop, and a bucket.

TIME FOR TOAST!
Try drawing this cute toaster.

Start with a rectangle with rounded corners.

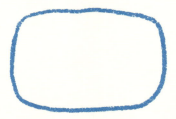

Then give it depth by adding the top and sides.

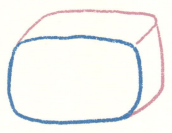

Draw the two slots in the top and the lever on the side. Add three little feet.

Give it a friendly face and then draw two pieces of toast leaping out. Pop!

ACTIVITY: MAKE A MOVING PICTURE!

Make your image come to life before your eyes with this fun optical illusion toy.

1 Take the press out magic spinner card out of your kit.

2 Draw a picture of a mug on one side.

3 On the other side, draw a kawaii face.

4 Thread a piece of string through each end of the card.

5 Hold a string in each hand and pull them taut, then twirl them so the disk flips over fast.

6 You'll see the face appear on the mug!

SPOOKY & SWEET

Trick or treat! It's time to get spooky! Do you love to celebrate Halloween with costumes, decorations, and parties? If so, you'll find you can make lots of great kawaii art for the occasion. Creepy ghosts, witches, and monsters become cute with a kawaii twist!

In Japan, Halloween is a mixture of spooky festivities and kawaii culture. People love to cosplay (dress up) as their favorite manga, anime, and kawaii characters. There are even special Halloween themed cafés!

GHOULISH GET-TOGETHER

Eek! These scary pals are having a fun Halloween party. Add more to the scene:

A ghost with a bow
A spider with shoes on
A zombie cat

POTION PALS

This little witch needs a friend. Draw another witch on the other side of the cauldron. Remember to include a hat and a broomstick!

MONSTER MASH

When you draw kawaii monsters, you can let your imagination run wild! They can be any shape and have lots of legs, extra eyes, crazy hair, whatever you want! Add another scary monster to this gang.

ACTIVITY: SPOOKY BUNTING

Make your room look cute and spooky with this cool decoration.

1 Find the press-out card marked Spooky Bunting. Draw your own designs on the blank pieces. You could include ghosts and bats, or pumpkins and witches.

2 Color them in. Then press them out of the card and thread them onto a string.

3 Hang it up around your room. Super spooky!

MAKING CHARACTERS

Now that you know how to make your art look kawaii, it's time to create some characters of your own! Draw some doodles and play around with ideas, letting your imagination run wild.

BUILD YOUR CHARACTER

You could draw a person, an animal, or even an object with a cute face. Think about some of the things you've already drawn and choose the one you like best. Then try out different hairstyles, poses, and accessories.

PERSONALITIES

Kawaii characters can have different personalities which are expressed through their poses and expressions. Think about what makes your character's personality unique! Maybe they are grumpy and always have a cute frown on their face. Perhaps they are shy and try to hide!

Now find the blank-face character sheets from your kit. Use your stencil to give each character an expression on their face. Then give each character a name that suits their personality.

FAIRY-TALE KAWAII

Another way to find kawaii character inspiration is by drawing some people or animals from a story you already know. For example, how about a cute kawaii version of Little Red Riding Hood, Cinderella, or Alice in Wonderland?

ACTIVITY: PUPPET TIME!

When you have drawn some characters you are happy with, you can bring them to life! Find the puppet press-out sheets in your kit. Draw your character designs on the blank puppet pieces and color them in. When your puppets are ready to go, stick them onto a popsicle stick or spare pencil, and let the fun begin! (One set of characters has already been drawn for you)

35

BACKGROUNDS & BACKDROPS

It's time to make the theater for your puppets to perform in! An interesting backdrop will bring your theater to life. It sets the scene for your characters and helps immerse your audience in the world you have created.

Your kit comes with one scene already drawn.

Turn the piece around to add your own scene on the back.

How about drawing a scene from Little Red Riding Hood? You might draw Little Red Riding Hood on her way to Granny's house. Draw lots of trees and pretty flowers, and a path leading to Granny's little cottage.

If you like princess stories, you could draw a mysterious palace or castle, which could be used for plays such as Cinderella or Beauty and the Beast.

Remember you can always make extra scenes from plain paper to add to your theater set. Keep them kawaii by using rounded shapes and simple lines. Color your backgrounds in using pastel or rainbow colors.

MAKE YOUR THEATER

Now that you have your character and scenes, it's time to put on a play!

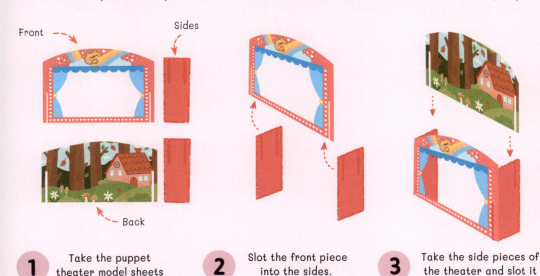

1 Take the puppet theater model sheets from your kit.

2 Slot the front piece into the sides.

3 Take the side pieces of the theater and slot it into the back piece.

NOW IT'S SHOWTIME!

Hold the puppets by their sticks or pencils and lower them into the theater. Have fun putting on a play for your family and friends!

Don't forget—you can always make more backdrops to change the scene!

DETAILS & DECORATIONS

Accessories are a fun way to express your personal style. Maybe you have a favorite hat, sunglasses, or hair clips that really finish your look. It's the same for your kawaii character! When you've drawn a cute character, you can show more of their personality by adding a few extra details. Decorations are also added to the backgrounds of the art and sometimes onto characters' bodies to make them look more fun and interesting.

MAKE IT FANCY!

Look at these classic kawaii decorations and add some more to the doughnut and cupcake scene below.

Bow   Rainbow   Hair clips

Popsicles and ice creams   Clouds   Candy

CHARM-A-LLAMA

Kawaii artists often use decorations called charms to add to their designs. These include things like stars, circles, flowers, and abstract shapes. They can be drawn onto the characters themselves and also around the image.
Try drawing charms onto this sassy llama!

ACCESSORIZE AND SHINE

Kawaii characters often have signature accessories that they carry—these might tell you something about their personality. Try copying these onto Emiko the bear and her friend.

Hats (beret and beanie)

Giant bow

Pets

Sunglasses

Umbrella

Lots of hair clips

ACTIVITY: DOODLE AND DECORATE!

Take the printed sheets from your kit. Now decorate each character with some of the charms, accessories, and embellishments you have learned to draw here. Then try out the stencils, and add some of the stickers to some extra cute details.

COLOR PALETTES

Let's take a look at how colors can be put together to create different effects. Primary colors are red, yellow, and blue. You can mix these together to create secondary colors.

Blue and red make purple.

Yellow and blue make green.

Red and yellow make orange.

When you mix the secondary colors with primary colors, you can create tertiary colors.

Here, all the colors are shown together on a color wheel.

SPIN THE WHEEL!

Color these two bears in complementary colors.

Complementary colors are two colors that lie directly across from each other on a color wheel. So why do complementary colors look great together? It's because they are opposite hues, one warm and one cool. For example: Yellow and purple; blue and orange; red and green. One makes the other appear brighter, and that way they both become more eye-catching.

FEEL THE RAINBOW

Colors can have an effect on the way we feel! Bright colors can be energizing, lighter colors can be soothing. How do these colors make you feel?

RED
excitement, danger

GREEN
nature, sickliness, envy

BLUE
relaxation, coldness, peace

YELLOW
warmth, friendliness

GRAY
cleanliness, innocence

PINK
pretty, playfulness, compassion

Kawaii art often uses pastel colors. These are considered to be light, soft, and calming. They make us feel happy and uplifted.

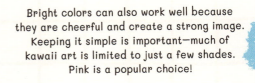

Bright colors can also work well because they are cheerful and create a strong image. Keeping it simple is important—much of kawaii art is limited to just a few shades. Pink is a popular choice!

ACTIVITY: COLOR COMPARISON

To understand the effect of different color palettes, try coloring the same picture in two different ways. Take the coloring sheets from your kit. Then follow the instructions to color by numbers. You can use colored pencils, crayons, or pens. One is in simple pastel shades. The other is in a wider range of colors, including some darker shades. What do you think of the results? Does it make a difference to how the picture makes you feel?

KAWAII CREATIONS: MAKE IT MOVE!

It's time for your own creative project—a cool kawaii flip book! A flip book is a series of images that change just slightly from one page to the next. When you flick through the pages qiuickly, it looks like they are animated.

SIMPLE STORY

Flip books usually feature a simple story with a twist! In our example, there seems to be a flower growing taller and taller. Then we see it's actually a cute mole popping up to say hello! Remember, keep your pictures simple—you will need to draw them 12 times.

Your kit contains printed sheets of paper that you can use to make your book. Cut out each rectangle carefully. Stack the papers on top of each other.

Before you start drawing on the flip book, practice on some scrap paper first, so you know exactly what you want to draw.

A flower is in a garden.

It begins to grow . . .

. . . and grow . . .

. . . and grow!

Something begins to appear!

We see its ears.

We see its eyes.

We see its nose.

It's a mole!

The mole blinks.

The mole opens its eyes.

The mole smiles.

When you're finished, put your pictures in a neat stack, then fasten them on the left with a staple or a paper clip. Now flip through and watch the story come to life!

KAWAII CREATIONS: PEEKABOO!

Show off your drawing skills by making your most detailed picture of all! This will be a fun hide-and-seek scene with as many different characters as possible. Get sneaky and hide some surprises for people to find.

Take the printed sheet from your kit. This has a bit of background detail on it to start you off. Now you need to add some funny pictures. Look at these suggestions and add your own great ideas!

SILLY SQUIRREL

This squirrel has an acorn for a hat! Start with a round face and add a small body. Give her little rounded ears. The tail is important—make it big and swirly. Now add the face and the acorn.

GREEDY FOX

This fox has a huge ice cream! Start with the head. Add the body and legs. Give him big pointy ears and a tail. Draw the ice cream. Then add the surprised expression!

SLEEPY PENGUIN

This little penguin has nodded off in the sunshine! Draw the shape of the body. Pop a pillow under her head. Add little feet and a spike of hair. Give her sleepy eyes and a beak. Add some zzz's. Sweet dreams!

FROGGIES AWAY!

A big balloon is lifting this little frog off the ground! Draw the body with head integrated, making sure to include semicircles for the bulging eyes. Add legs hanging down, and small arms holding the string. Draw the heart-shaped balloon up above her. Add a frown and some blushing cheeks.

AXOLOTL SEES STARS

A ball has bounced off this axolotl's head! Make the head bigger than the body. Draw the feathery gills. Add stars for eyes and a wide mouth. Show the soccer bouncing off his head with some little movement marks. Poor axolotl!

SHY HEDGEHOG

This hedgehog is hiding. She's trying to be brave, but she's feeling a bit shy! First draw the object she's hiding behind—it could a tree, a chair, or something else entirely! Then draw her cute little face peeking out.

KAWAII CREATIONS: MAKE IT POP!

Mai the Sloth says, "Come on in, the water is warm!" Use the skills you've learned to make a pop-up featuring Mai and her friend on a sunny trip to the seaside.

SET THE SCENE

Find the pop-up scene modelling card in your kit and fold along the dotted line. Push out the three tabs so they pop-up at right angles when the card is opened, as shown in the picture. Each tab has a differed colored dot to show you where to glue each pop-up pal.

BEACH SLOTHS

1
The three pop-up images are provided for you, so you just need to color them in and then attach them to the scene. Glue Mai the sloth in the pool floatie to the pop-up tab with a red dot.

2
The next pop-up is a kawaii bucket filled with sand. Glue the bucket to the tab with the yellow dot.

46

3

The biggest pop-up shows a sloth on a lounge chair. Glue this sloth to the tab with the blue dot.

4

Now try closing your scene, making sure that everything folds down properly. You might need to press around some of the folds to make sure it is really neat and flat.

POP TIME!

Open it out and proudly display your kawaii beach scene!

© 2025 Quarto Publishing plc

Author: Ellen Philpott
Illustrator: Ilaria Ranauro
Editors: Hannah Cockayne and Amber Jones
Designer: Melissa Gandhi

First published in 2025 by Design Eye, an imprint of The Quarto Group.
100 Cummings Center, Suite 265D, Beverly, MA 01915, USA
T +1 978-282-9590 F +1 078-283-2742

www.quarto.com

No part of this publication may be reproduced, stored in a retrieval system, or transmitted in any form, or by any means, electrical, mechanical, photocopying, recording or otherwise, without the prior written permission of the publisher or a licence permitting restricted copying. In the United Kingdom such licences are issued by the Copyright Licensing Agency, 5th Floor, Shackleton House, 4 Battle Bridge Lane, London SE1 2HX.

All rights reserved.

A catalogue record for this book is available from the British Library.

ISBN: 978-1-83600-532-2

Image Credits
Alamy Picture Library; page 4: Katarzyna Soszka: lm;
Sean Pavone: m; Imageplotter News and Sports: bl;
Feije Riemersma: rm

Every attempt has been made to clear the copyright. Should there be any inadvertent omission, please apply to the publisher for rectification.

Manufactured in Shaoguan, China
SL042025

9 8 7 6 5 4 3 2 1